The Magic Bicycle

Written by
John Townsend

Illustrated by
Shirley Chiang

We all loved Miss Asan. She often rode her old bike down our road. She always waved as she sped past.

Her bike would rattle, her basket would wobble and her wheels would squeak. But that didn't matter. Her bike was magic.

I knew that Miss Asan could make her bike fly! I'd see her ride past and then she'd be gone. With three rings of her bell, her bike would soar over the trees.

A tiny dot moved over the rooftops – a sari flapping in the wind.

People said it was a big bird gliding in the sky. But I knew it was Miss Asan on her magic bike.

I once asked her, "Can your bike really fly, Miss Asan?"

She smiled at me with a wink.

"Of course. I flew across India on it. But *shsh*, it's a secret."

Miss Asan was almost ninety years old.

One day she rode past me and waved to me.

"I'm off to take my rava cakes to the old folks."

She was always taking cakes to people.

I heard her bell. It rang three times. Then her bike rose into the sky and her sari flapped behind her.

Soon she was no more than a speck in the clouds. Magic!

Yes, we all loved Miss Asan. She was so kind and such fun.

Sadly the day came when she said, "I'm too old to ride my bike now. I'm going to sell it. I'd like someone else to use my magic bike to help others."

She put an advert in the shop window:

BARGAIN BUYS

Old bike for sale. It needs love.
Use it for doing good.
For the right person, it will fly!

I heard Mrs Brown next door.

"I want to fly. I don't care about doing good. I just want something that no one else has. And I *always* get what I want."

She stamped her foot. "I will turn that old heap of rust into a smart, new super-bike. I'll whizz over people's heads. I'll make them *so* jealous. You just see."

Sure enough, Mrs Brown got that bike.

"I can't wait to make it my own," she said.

In just a few days, the bike had shiny new wheels.

Mrs Brown had big plans.

"That bike needs a new frame. I'll keep the bell. That's all. That's the magic bit."

She got rid of the basket on the front. She fixed a bigger saddle as well (for her big bottom).

Soon the bike was nothing like it used to be.

Mrs Brown rode the bike with her nose in the air. She never waved as she sped past. There was no basket to wobble and the wheels were silent.

The only sound was the bell. She never stopped ringing it.

The bike never rose into the sky. Not even once. It didn't soar over the trees.

All we heard was Mrs Brown shouting.

"You stupid bike. You're no good. You're not magic at all!"

She kicked its wheels. She hit it with the pump and the chain fell off.

The bike was never the same again.

It ended up in a shed covered in cobwebs. All the magic had gone forever.

The moral of this little story is – if something works just fine, don't meddle with it. After all, if it isn't broken, why try to fix it?

Sometimes the old ways really are the best ways.

As Mrs Brown found out!